HELPER HOUNDS

Spooky

Helps Danny Tell the Truth

Dedication
To Rafi, Henrik, Greta, and Fredrik

To the courthouse dogs
Thank you for good work you do

HELPER HOUNDS

Spooky

Helps Danny Tell the Truth

Caryn Rivadeneira
Illustrated by Priscilla Alpaugh

RED CHAIR
·PRESS·

Egremont, Massachusetts

RED CHAIR PRESS
BOOKS FOR YOUNG READERS
www.redchairpress.com

 Free educator's guide at www.redchairpress.com/free-resources

Publisher's Cataloging-In-Publication Data

Names: Rivadeneira, Caryn Dahlstrand, author. | Alpaugh, Priscilla, illustrator.

Title: Spooky helps Danny tell the truth / Caryn Rivadeneira ; illustrated by Priscilla Alpaugh.

Description: Egremont, Massachusetts : Red Chair Press, [2020] | Series: Helper hounds ; [book 6] | Interest age level: 006-009. | Includes facts about American Staffordshire terriers. | Summary: "Danny is scared to tell the truth. After he saw someone steal some bikes, now he has to see that person in a courtroom and tell the court what he did. To help calm Danny's fears on the big day, his parents call the Helper Hounds-and there's no better pup for the job than Spooky. Spooky was involved in a crime herself-she lost her leg after being shot by a police officer who thought she was dangerous. The officer learned from his mistake and became a better person, and he thinks Danny can do the same for the bike thief. Will Spooky's best calming tricks, like stretching and yoga, give Danny the courage to tell the truth in court-and to help change the thief's life for the better?"-- Provided by publisher.

Identifiers: ISBN 9781634409179 (hc) | ISBN 9781634409209 (sc) | ISBN 9781634409230 (ebook)

Subjects: LCSH: American Staffordshire terrier--Juvenile fiction. | Child witnesses--Juvenile fiction. | Honesty--Juvenile fiction. | Anxiety--Juvenile fiction. | CYAC: Dogs--Fiction. | Witnesses--Fiction. | Honesty--Fiction. | Anxiety--Fiction.

Classification: LCC PZ7.1.R57627 Sp 2021 (print) | LCC PZ7.1.R57627 (ebook) | DDC [E]--dc23

Library of Congress Control Number: 2020937700

Photos: iStock

Printed in the United States of America

0920 1P CGS21

CHAPTER 1

I leaned on my front foot while Reg lifted a back one. He wriggled my foot into the boot and then set it down.

"Next paw, Spooky," Reg said and tapped my leg. He slipped my paw into the boot and set it down. Reg patted my bottom and looked me over. My goggles were set. My lab coat was buttoned. My three boots all on.

"Lookin' good," Reg said.

My tail whipped back and forth. I knew I looked good. With my sleek gray coat and my wide happy smile, it was hard not to. Especially when I was in my lab gear.

We left Reg's office and trotted down the hallway toward the lab. As we walked, students smiled and waved hello. Alisa stopped us just outside the lab.

"Morning, Prof. Boot," Alisa said.

"Morning," Reg said. "And yes, you may pet Spooky."

Alisa smiled and knelt to greet me. She pushed her lips into a kissy face as she said my name slowly, "Spoooooooooooky."

Since she made her face so nicely, I kissed her right on the lips. The leftover spice from her taco lunch tasted as good as it smelled.

"I miss being in your class," Alisa said. "Prof. Lester is less than…"

Reg cleared his throat.

Alisa looked up. Prof. Lester had stepped out of the classroom and stood beside me.

"Reginald, Alisa, Spooky," Prof. Lester said with a nod to each of us.

My butt wriggled harder at the sound of my name—and the sight of Prof. Lester.

Prof. Lester didn't smile at or fuss over me as much as some people did. She was an astronomer and more of a "star person" than dog person. Prof. Lester said she could tell when stars—and apparently dogs—were special and worth paying attention to. And when Prof. Lester first met me, she said she liked my "moxie" and that I was a star. I didn't know what moxie meant or much about stars, but that was good to hear.

"Morning, Prof. Lester," Alisa said.

"Morning, Marcia," Reg said.

"Any new cases?" Prof. Lester said.

"Matter of fact, I just got a text," Reg said. "Looks like Spooky will be heading to court."

Prof. Lester gave me a small smile and a wink. Then, she turned to leave. But not before she reached down for a quick scratch of my head. "Good dog," she whispered. "Brightest star around."

Alisa looked at her phone. "Shoot," she said. "Late for class!"

Alisa kissed the top of my head. I tried to get one more lick of the taco spice, but she was too fast.

"All right, Spooky," Reg said. "We need to get to class too. I gotta check my email, see what this new case is all about."

Reg adjusted my lab coat and opened the door. I followed him in. He let go of my leash as soon as we got in the room. I knew the drill. Reg headed for his teaching table at the front of the lab. I hopped toward my bed in the corner.

Every Monday, Wednesday, and Friday, while Reg taught chemistry to the students, I slept in my lab gear. Even though I never touched the chemicals in the laboratory, the rules were that everyone in the lab must wear safety equipment. Including dogs!

Reg didn't need to bring me to class, but he thought it was good practice for me. And it was! As a Helper Hound, sometimes I have to put on extra equipment. And I had to get used to all sorts of strange places and people doing weird things. If you ask me, there aren't many places stranger or people weirder than humans in white coats and goggles mixing potions in beakers in a chemistry lab.

As the students filed into the room, most gave me a scratch or two behind the goggles. As soon as Reg started his lecture, I nodded off (along with a couple of the students). Sometimes the clinking of beakers would wake me up. But most of the time, I didn't wake up until the students were shuffling out of the room.

It was the same on this day. Class—and my nap—were over. And not a moment too soon. We had a new Helper Hounds case after all.

"I just read the full email," Reg said as he knelt beside me in his office and unbuttoned my coat and slid off my boots and goggles. "A kid named Danny saw someone steal some bikes. Now, he has to go to court to testify. He was actually just in court last year when he got adopted, but he's really nervous about having to say what he saw. Judge Mathers thinks you can help."

I barked at the word help. Of course, I could help. That's what Helper Hounds do!

"What do you think? Should we say yes?"

I barked again. Not that I ever said no to Helper Hounds cases, but once upon a time, I saw someone commit a crime. Actually, I was the victim of the crime. I had to go to court for that too. Also, I know we don't act our best when we feel scared. Learning to relax is very, very important. Let me tell you the story of how I know all this.

CHAPTER 2

Tina Thornton was right the day they first spotted me in the shelter: they didn't have time for a dog. But I was just so cute and hard to resist, and Tina thought maybe I'd make a good companion, so she gave in to her boys' begging to adopt me.

The Thorntons were really nice, and Tina's boys were great at playing with me and sneaking me leftover snacks. But Tina worked long hours, and the boys were either at school or sports practice or outside playing.

That meant, I had lots of time on my own. When I got bored (which happened a lot), I'd check the back door. The boys left it unlocked all the time.

It didn't take too long for me to learn that all I needed was one good nose-nudge, and the door would bounce open. At least, open enough for me to sneak my snout in and push myself out.

This was about the time I began to develop Life Rules. My first Life Rule was: Push yourself! You can do more than you think you can!

When I'd push myself—and that door— all my boredom disappeared. The world was mine! I would explore the back alleys and chase squirrels and cats. I'd knock over garbage cans and sniff around for leftover sandwiches and pie crusts. I'd head to the playground and run with the kids. I'd know it was time to go home when the police came to get me.

The police officers who came for me would whistle or call me by name (they learned it quickly!). When I came running, the police

officers would give me a treat
and pet me while I rolled
over on my belly. Then
they'd take me for a ride
back home in the squad car.
As they drove, I'd slip and
slide all over the backseat.
Good times.

The officers would bring
me to the front door. If Tina
answered, they'd remind her it was against the
law to let a dog run loose. She'd apologize and
then promise to fix the back lock. If the boys
answered, they'd get told to help their mom and
keep a better eye on me. If no one answered,
they'd let me back inside through the back
door. Somehow, they also learned that door was
always open.

But nothing much changed. The cycle would
always repeat: Tina and the boys would leave

the house, I'd get bored, I'd go have some fun, and my police friends would bring me home.

Until one day, one bad day. Until, the day I got shot!

I'd seen the lights and heard the sounds of shouting a few doors down. So, I pushed the door open and ran out to investigate. I trotted out of our yard and right down the block.

That's when I saw them: my police friends! Officer Lester and Officer Jackson stood by two officers I didn't recognize. I paused for a moment to sniff the air. My friends were really focused on the front door of a house. Some officers were shouting. Others just held their guns straight and still. Something bad was happening in that house. The officers were all tense. I could tell. The air smelled like panic.

An officer yelled something toward the house. I picked up my trot again. I thought I could help! A good belly scratch for me always calms everyone down! My trot turned into a gallop.

Galloping toward the officers turned out to be a mistake.

Because as I ran toward Officer Lester, a police officer from the other side of the yard yelled, "Pit bull! Look out!"

Now, I should pause and tell you I'm technically a Staffordshire terrier, which is a pit-bull-type dog. People cry "pit bull" for all sorts of dogs even if we aren't officially American pit bull terriers. But this really doesn't matter, so I'll continue with the story.

Officer Lester and the cop I didn't know turned to look. Then, two things happened at once.

Officer Lester put her gun down and yelled, "Spoooooooky! Stop!"

And the officer I didn't know turned toward me, gun still drawn. A wave of panic-smell roared toward me. The man was terrified—of me!

Before I could put on my brakes, I heard Officer Lester yell, "NOOOOOO!"

Then the officer I didn't know pulled the trigger.

The bad news? I got shot. Right in the leg.

The good news? I don't remember much about it. Not the pain. Not getting wrapped in

a blanket by Officer Jackson and Officer Lester. Not getting rushed to the vet. I wish I did remember this because I got to ride up front for once—right on Officer Lester's lap!

No, the next thing I knew, I was lying on a cold table with a warm blanket on me. I wriggled my nose. Something was in it: a tube! My ears started picking up sounds around me. A man sniffled beside me.

I stretched and moaned. Then the sniffling man said, "She's waking up!"

People shuffled all around me. I blinked my eyes open and watched a blur of people gather around me. Some wore white jackets. Others wore blue uniforms. The sniffling man wore blue. I noticed the sparkle of his badge right away.

The room smelled like poodle poop and cat pee with an under-whiff of Lysol.

But there was another, familiar smell. Something from just earlier in the day: gun metal and panic.

"Spooky," a voice said. "Good to see you, buddy."

I recognized the voice: Officer Lester!

I sniffed around the tube in my nose and tried to lift my head. There was that familiar panic smell again. This time the smell came right to my nose as the sniffling man leaned in to rest his head on my shoulder.

"I am so, so sorry, Spooky," he said. "I am so sorry."

The familiar smell reminded me of one of my favorite smells: bacon. Turns out, the officer had a nice spot of grease on his sleeve. I leaned in for a lick.

"She kissed you," the woman in the white coat said. "Looks like she accepts your apology."

Now, humans have a bad habit of reading too much into dogs' "kisses." Sometimes we are just trying to lick the last bits of peanut butter off your messy faces! But other times, trying to get a lick of bacon grease paves the way for love and understanding.

That's what happened with me and Officer Torres—the officer who shot me.

Because that day wasn't only the beginning of a new life for me, it was the beginning of a new life for Officer Torres.

CHAPTER 3

Let me make a long story short.

As soon as he pulled the trigger, Officer Torres knew he made a huge mistake. Later, when he visited schools, Officer Torres would tell students that he let his nerves and his prejudice and fear of pit bulls (again, I'm technically a Staffordshire terrier) get the best of him. His fear and prejudice affected his judgement. Those things caused him to make a terrible mistake. He wanted to do better.

So, Officer Torres turned in his gun and took time off from being a cop. He saw doctors and therapists. He took classes in meditation and yoga. All to help him calm down and control his nerves.

While Officer Torres was learning to handle his nerves better, I had to learn to walk better. The bullet shattered a bone in my front leg. The vets decided the best option was to amputate—or take off!—my whole leg. Turned out, they were right. I barely even noticed my leg was gone.

And after several days in the hospital, Officer Lester became my foster mom. That meant, she'd take care of me until I found a new forever home. I wasn't going back to live with Tina and her boys. After my final escape, Tina realized her home wasn't safe for me. She was right. Even though I missed Tina's boys, Officer Lester always had something to keep me busy. She took me to therapy where I practiced walking on a treadmill in the water. She took me to obedience classes, where I did a great

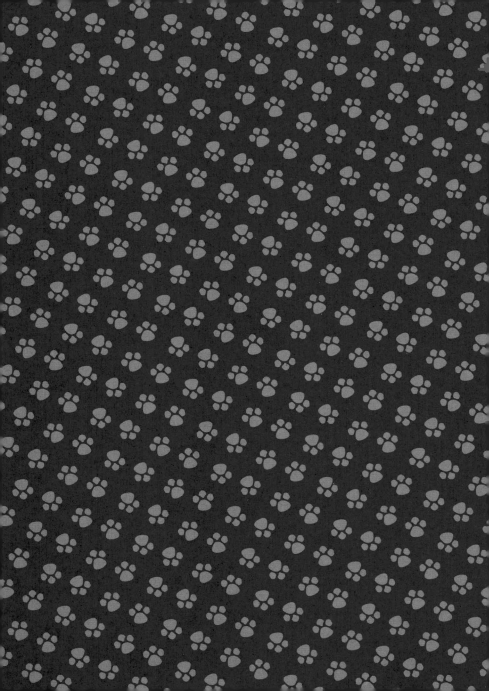

job with all kinds of commands and tricks. She took me on long walks through the forest preserve. Officer Lester let me stretch with (and sometimes climb on) her when she did her morning yoga. But Officer Lester also worked long hours and had to have people come let me out when she was away. So, her home wasn't a permanent solution either.

One day, when Officer Lester's sister offered to take me to visit the college where she taught. I thought it was just for fun. But Officer Lester's sister had other plans. Prof. Lester heard all about my story, my recovery, and how well I was doing in obedience class. Officer Lester's sister was extra impressed when she heard I showed up at court to visit Officer Torres—and that I snuggled right up next to him as the judge told him he was ready to be a cop again. That's when she first noticed my moxie. So, Prof. Lester took me to campus and walked right up to an office door.

"Let's introduce you to Reg," Prof. Lester whispered as we stopped in front of a door. And that's when my life really changed.

Prof. Lester knocked on the office door. A man in a white lab coat opened it, smiled, and knelt right down to say hi to me. I slurped his nose. He smiled and sniffled. His eyes smelled like salt.

"Prof. Boot," Prof. Lester said. "This is Spooky. You may have seen her on the news. She was shot. By a police officer."

"Hi Spooky, I'm Reg…Reginald Boot. And I did hear about you," Reg said, as he scratched me all over. I rolled onto my back, so he could get to my belly better.

"She's remarkable. My sister was on duty the day Spooky was shot. She saw the whole thing— rushed Spooky to the vet. She's fostering her now."

"Oh, yeah?" Reg asked. "Is she working with her?"

"Quite a bit," Prof. Lester said. "She takes her to physical therapy and obedience classes. Spooky really excels at obedience—and at people skills, as you can see."

I was sitting in Reg's lap by now, staring up at him and slurping his face.

"Spooky holds no grudges," Prof. Lester says. "She went to court with Officer Torres—the man who shot her—and helped him testify about what happened. Remarkable. As you know, my dream is to discover a new star, and I believe I have. Prof. Boot, I have found your next Helper Hound."

Reg smiled at me but shook his head. His eyes got glossy and began to smell of salt again.

"I'm just not sure I'm ready to go through it again," Reg said. He wiped his face, so I licked it for him. "I still miss Rico so much."

Prof. Boot sunk his face into my shoulder. The nice thing about missing a leg is that you have more spaces to snuggle.

"What would make Rico happier than to know you got another Helper Hound—to carry on his legacy? Besides, rescuing—and loving—another dog is the best thing for grief—and your life. You know it."

Reg flipped his university name badge over and showed me a picture of a brindle Staffordshire Terrier. He looked a lot like me—if I were part tiger.

"This was my Rico," Reg said. "He was a Helper Hound. He died a couple months ago. I miss him."

I sniffed the picture—a faint scent of rubbing alcohol—and then snuggled tighter into Reg. He smelled sad. I wanted to help.

"She's very responsive," Reg said.

Prof. Lester nodded. "I'm telling you. She's the one."

Apparently, Reg agreed. Because before I knew it, Reg adopted me. I became Spooky Boot! We moved my dog bed and food into Reg's little house and headed off to Helper Hounds University. Because I only had three legs, I had to work extra hard on some of the tricks and skills Helper Hounds needed to know. But I figured it out. Plus, Mr. Tuttle, the founder of Helper Hounds, thought only having three legs would make me a better Helper Hound. It would help others relate to me, he said.

All I know is that my new life was looking great. After several months of training, I got my red vest and name badge and became an official Helper Hound.

Who could've imagined all this back when I was escaping out of back doors or when I was on that operating table?

As they say, all things turn out for the best—and it's true! Now, let's get back to Danny.

CHAPTER 4

I stretched my front leg forward and my snout toward the sky. I held the pose until Reg took my vest off the hook and brought it to me.

"You should teach doggy yoga—doga," Reg laughed to himself as he snapped my vest on. "Never can get over your balance and flexibility."

Reg said this to me whenever I practiced my poses. I do have good balance—and flexibility. So it is nice to show it off a bit. But really, I just love to stretch. Stretching feels so good and is so relaxing. Whenever we head out on a new Helper Hounds case or a day at school, I make sure to stretch as long and deep as I can. In fact, my second Life Rule is: S T R E T C H yourself. It's good to really feel your muscles work. I can do anything after a good stretch.

I stood up straight as Reg snapped my vest and leash on. My tail swooshed back and forth. We were ready to go.

• • •

Reg and I stood at the bottom of a steep stack of white stairs.

"You okay with all these stairs, Spooky?" Reg asked.

I answered by hopping up two steps at a time.

The revolving doors to the courthouse gave me a little pause. There's a weird rhythm and flow to those things. It's hard to coordinate on my three legs. But I did fine. When we stepped out of the doors, Reg took off my vest and set it on the conveyor belt. A security guard told me to stop and stay. Then she called me through the metal detector. They took a wand and ran it all over my body. It beeped at my tags, but the guard didn't seem worried. As Reg snapped my vest back on, I noticed a boy staring at me across the hall. He tugged at a woman's coattail and pointed.

The woman turned to follow the boy's point and smiled broadly. She tapped the man standing next to her.

Soon, the little family was walking right at us.

"You must be Spooky," the woman said.

My butt shook at the sound of my name.

The man and woman stood up close; the boy tucked in behind them.

"Yes," Reg said. "This is Spooky. You must be Danny."

Reg peeked around the grown-ups. Danny pressed his face into the woman's coat but nodded.

"I'm Caroline, and this is Ben," the woman

said. They shook hands. Ben leaned down to pet me. I sprawled on the floor, so I could get a better look at the kid behind Caroline's legs. "And yes, this is Danny back here. The courthouse isn't his favorite place."

"Mine either, Danny," Reg said. "I prefer my chemistry lab."

"I have a chemistry set," came a small voice from behind Caroline.

"Oh yeah?" Reg said. "What do you like to do with it?"

"Mix stuff," the voice said. "And make bubbles."

"Do you wear goggles and gloves when you mix stuff and make bubbles?" Reg asked.

"Yes," the voice said. "Mama Caroline makes me."

"Smart lady," Reg said. "Wanna see a picture of Spooky in her goggles?"

Reg held out his phone. I sat up as Danny

peeked around to see.

Danny giggled and then smiled at me.

"She lets you put those on?"

Reg nodded. "I brought some with me. Want me to show you how we do it?"

Danny nodded again.

"Actually, can you help me?"

Danny slowly moved from behind Caroline. Reg reached into his messenger bag and pulled

out my goggles. I stood up and started wiggling. I didn't know they had a lab in this place! Then I remembered: Sometimes Reg had me put on goggles to show people how good I was or how goofy I looked. I was never quite sure.

Danny giggled when he saw my ears flipped up above the rubber band.

"I might've gotten better than a D in chemistry if I had this girl in my class," Ben said.

Caroline shook her head. "You might've gotten better than a D if you would have cracked open your textbook!" she said.

"Spooky helps students relax," Reg said. "But she can't help them pass if they don't study."

"True," Ben said as he looked at his watch. "Judge Mathers and the district attorney are expecting us. We should head down there."

Danny's body stiffened. His face grew hard. Danny shook his head and stared down the long marble corridor. Once again, I smelled the sharp scent of panic. But Danny wasn't afraid of me. He was afraid of whatever—or whomever—waited down the long marble hallway.

I stepped closer to Danny as he stared into space. I licked his hand. He still didn't move.

"Danny, honey, Judge Mathers and DA Donaldson are very kind," Caroline said. "You have nothing to worry about. Today is just a simple meeting."

Danny didn't move.

Caroline and Ben looked at each other. Then they looked at Reg.

Reg smiled and knelt down in front of Danny.

"Want to see what Spooky does when she gets nervous?" Reg asked.

Danny turned toward me, tilted his head, and nodded.

CHAPTER 5

Reg looked around the courthouse lobby. Then he handed my leash to Caroline and said, "Hold her, please. I'll be right back."

He walked up to a security guard and said something. The guard gave him a funny look but then shrugged his shoulders. The guard helped Reg carry three big rope barriers to where we stood.

"Can you help me?" Reg asked Danny. Danny nodded and held an end of one rope. Reg showed him how to connect it to another pole. Soon, we had blocked off a big triangle around where we stood.

"This way, we have some space," Reg said.

Danny turned around in the triangle. "For what?"

"A little yoga, er, doga," Reg said with a smile to himself.

"Doga? Like, doggy yoga? Here? Now?" Ben asked.

"Absolutely," said Reg. "Spooky always gets a good stretch in before we do anything. That's what she does when she's nervous. And you know what? She's on to something. Good stretches calm us. There's a science to it, actually. I could tell you about the chemistry of that when we have more time."

"That's okay," Danny said. "I just want to see."

Reg pulled his hand up to a sit command. Then he waved his hand down. I lay down. Then Reg stretched his arms wide. I pushed myself back up. My front leg held stick straight.

My back legs angled toward the floor. Once again, my snout reached high into the sky. For the first time I noticed the giant dome above us. Light streamed in through the windows all around it.

"Good girl," Reg said.

I shook it all off and sat back down.

"Why does she do that?" Danny asked.

"I can't tell you for sure," Reg said. "But I notice she does it just before we leave the house on every Helper Hounds case. I think it relaxes her."

"How does she do it without that leg?"

"After she lost her leg, she worked really hard to get strong again." Reg said. "Stretching and exercise were part of that."

Danny nodded. "So maybe Spooky feels nervous and then she stretches and feels better?"

"I feel better—stronger even—after I go to yoga," Ben said.

"Me too," Reg said and turned to Danny. "Wanna try some stretches with Spooky?"

"Right here? With the people walking by?" Danny asked.

"Why not?" Reg said. "They probably could use some relaxing lessons too."

Before Reg could even ask, I struck my pose again. Front leg straight. Back legs angled. Snout straight to the dome.

Danny scrambled onto the ground, lifted one arm up, stretched his toes all the way back, and turned his face to the dome.

"It's not fair if I balance on two arms and two legs if Spooky can only balance on three," Danny said.

"That's nice of you," Reg said. "But Spooky's okay with you using all four if it helps. Spooky would use her other leg if she had it!"

Caroline snapped a picture before Danny put his arm down.

"Don't post that," Danny said. "Not till I get better at balancing."

"I won't," Caroline said. "But later you'll want to see how cute the two of you look practicing."

And apparently, we did look cute. Because lots of other people stopped to watch us. Some snapped pictures, and Reg politely asked them not to post anything. You never know if they'll listen. People get pretty excited when they see a Helper Hound out in "the wild."

I've also gotten good at ignoring the looky-loos who try to get glimpses of Helper Hounds at work. So, I ignored everyone and focused only on Danny. As he stretched his head up, I went back into my pose. Together, we stretched. Side by side. Body by body. I could hear his heartbeat slowing down.

But then someone walked by with a breakfast burrito. I caught one quick whiff, and I decided to practice another of my life rules: Stop to Sniff the Air. There's just something about a long deep sniff that somehow calms the jitters and tells us all is right with the world—what with all its interesting smells. And that proved true again as I took a long, deep sniff of the scrambled egg and sausage and peppery cheese....

Danny noticed my deep sniffing and added

a deep breath of his own. Now he was really getting the hang of it!

I held my stretch two more quick sniffs and then shook it off. Danny looked over at me and did the same. We both stood up.

Reg moved the ropes back by the security guard and said, "I think our yoga session is probably over."

"How you feeling?" Caroline asked.

Danny smiled. "Much better!" He put his hand over his heart. "My heart's not racing."

"Good news," Ben said. "You ready to go meet the judge and the district attorney?"

Danny closed his eyes, stretched his fingers, and took a deep breath.

"I'm ready," he said.

CHAPTER 6

Judge Mathers opened the door and immediately knelt down. Her robes bagged around her as she scratched my head.

"Excuse my manners," Judge Mathers said as she smushed her face into mine. "I know I should ask before I pet her. But I had a Staffordshire terrier like her when I was a girl. Mine was white with a black spot right on her eye. She looked like a panda."

Judge Mathers made bear claws with her hands and winked at Danny.

Danny looked at me and scrunched his eyebrows. "Spooky looks more like a hippo."

"She does!" Reg said. "And for what it's worth, the judge is right. Always ask before petting a strange dog. Of course, Helper Hounds have to be okay with people petting them—even without asking. The judge knows that," Reg added.

"I do!" Judge Mathers said. "In fact, it's why I wanted you to be here with Danny. He has to be very brave today, and I thought Spooky could help him."

Judge Mathers motioned her arm toward her office and stepped back, so we could walk in. Right away, I spotted a wide sofa along a wall of windows. Since there's nothing quite like being comfortable and being able to watch the world go by, I walked straight to the sofa and looked back longingly at Reg.

"She's very polite," Caroline said. "She's asking if she can climb up, isn't she?"

"She is," Reg said. "If we were at home,

or anywhere without her vest on, Spooky'd definitely climb right up and make herself comfortable. But when she's at work, Spooky knows better."

"Well, she's welcome to climb up," Judge Mathers said. "Perhaps Danny can sit next to her. I'll pull up chairs, so you and District Attorney Donaldson can talk."

While DA Donaldson introduced himself to everyone in the room and Judge Mathers excused herself, I climbed up on the sofa, took a quick peek out the windows to make sure no trouble was happening outside, and curled up. I put my big head right on Danny's lap. I could hear his heart beating—all the way down in his leg. When the DA pulled up his chair, Danny's heart beat faster and faster again. It was time to remind Danny of the tricks. I stretched my front legs way out and stuck my snout in the air for a good sniff. Danny stretched his legs beneath me and took a deep breath himself. His heartbeat slowed back down.

"Now," DA Donaldson said. "Today you're going to be called on to tell the truth. Another lawyer and I will ask you questions about what you saw, about what happened the day your bike was stolen. All you have to do is remember the best you can and answer their questions. You don't have to say more than they ask. It's really quite simple. And Spooky can sit with you the whole time."

"Even when I have to go up front?" Danny said.

"Even when you have to go up front," DA Donaldson said.

Danny looked straight down at me and gave my head long strokes.

"I understand you've been in court before," DA Donaldson said.

"When I got adopted," Danny said without taking his eyes off me.

"That must've been a happy day!" DA Donaldson said.

Danny nodded. Caroline and Ben smiled at each other.

"But he didn't have to go in that box then," Ben said. "He got to stay with Mama Caroline and Dad."

"I understand," DA Donaldson said. "And that's why Spooky is here. Spooky gets to go in the box—as you call it—with you. She can be with you the whole time. She's done this before, you know."

Danny stretched his legs and took a deep breath. "Yes," Danny said. "I know. But what about the guy?"

"The guy?" Judge Mathers asked. "Oh, the defendant? Yes, he will be there too. So that part also feels scary, I know."

Caroline reached forward to touch Danny's knee. "And not only is Spooky there, but we're in the room too," Caroline said. "The guy can't hurt you. He's the one who did something wrong."

"That's true," DA Donaldson said. "And think of it this way: In a courtroom, we tell and listen to lots of stories. And from those stories, the jury tries to determine what is the true story—what happened and what didn't. Your role today is very important in helping us get to the true story. Lots of kids have been getting their bikes stolen in town. There are lots of sad kids! You were already so brave to tell the police when you saw those bikes getting taken... especially since he scared you so much."

I felt Danny's heart beat faster.

"He still scares me," Danny said. "I still have bad dreams about the look he gave me when I saw him taking the bikes. I don't want to see him again."

Danny burst into tears, and I burst into action. I pressed my head deep into his chest. He hugged me tight.

Just then, there was a knock at the door.

"Come in," DA Donaldson said.

It was the court bailiff. "Trial is about to start," she said.

DA Donaldson stood up and we followed him out.

CHAPTER 7

Reg handed Danny my leash. Danny wiped his tears and then said, "You want me to walk Spooky?"

Reg nodded. "Spooky can feel you through the leash, did you know that? She can tell if you're relaxed or nervous or happy or sad. And if you try really hard, you can feel her too. Spooky's feeling pretty chill today and will be happy to send her chill up the leash."

Danny scrunched his eyebrows and shook his head. Then he grabbed the leash. Reg was right: I'm always happy to share my chill (it's actually a Life Rule!), so I did my best to send it up my leash to Danny.

"Wait," Danny said just before we walked out of the judge's office. "One more thing."

With my leash still in hand, Danny stretched out on the ornate rug. I followed suit. Then I rolled over and shook my legs in the air. Danny did the same.

Caroline, Ben, and Reg all laughed. The court bailiff did not. She held her arm into the hallway and tapped her watch. It was time to go. Together we walked toward the courtroom. I could hear Danny's deep breaths and feel his heart pounding. I gave Danny a huge smile and sent more chill up the leash. But then, a scent caught my nose.

I stopped dead in my tracks. So did Officer Torres.

"Spooky!" came a voice from behind Officer Torres.

My tail began to wag. Officer Lester!

"My sister told me you were going to be in court today. Was hoping I'd see you," Officer Lester said as she walked up. My wiggles were about to get the best of me, so I sat. If I weren't in my Helper Hounds vest, I'd have jumped into the lap Officer Lester created when she squatted in front of me. But I was working, so I just wiggled and wriggled in my sitting position.

"Spooky lived with Officer Lester after she got shot," Reg said. "She rescued her and got her walking again. It's because of her, and her sister, that Spooky's here with us now."

"And it's because of that guy that Spooky got shot," Danny said, his face hard as a rock.

"What?" Caroline asked, following Danny's finger.

"I read about it," Danny said. "I'd remember his face anywhere."

"Good memory," said Reg. "You are a good witness."

"Yes, you are," Officer Torres said.

I stood up as Officer Torres approached. My tail helicoptered round and round. My front foot took tiny leaps off the ground in my best three-legged bucking bronco impression.

"You're right, I am the guy who shot Spooky," Officer Torres said as he knelt down in front of me.

Danny watched as I licked Officer Torres all over his face and sniffed his shirt for the bacon grease. (I found a bit on the cuffs.)

"Why isn't Spooky scared of you?" Danny asked.

"Spooky is one brave and forgiving dog," Officer Torres said. "She's the reason I was able to get the help I needed and the reason I'm still a police officer today. Without her, something much worse might have happened in my life. But the day she showed up in court for me—and helped tell the story of what happened—changed my life. Seeing her go on and become a Helper Hound despite what I'd done to her made me a better man. She's a hero."

Danny looked at me and nodded.

"I have to tell a story today," Danny said.

"Oh yeah?" Officer Torres said. "You're a hero too?"

"Yeah," Danny said. "I saw a man steal some

bikes. He told me I better not tell anyone. But I did. I told my parents. They told the police. He got arrested. Now I have to see him today."

"You get to be Spooky today," Officer Torres said. "You get to help change someone's life by telling the truth now."

Officer Torres tapped Danny on the shoulder. Then he rubbed my belly. A voice came over the radio on Officer Torres' shoulder. He spoke into it and turned to Officer Lester.

"We gotta run," he said. "Duty calls." Officer Lester nodded.

The bailiff said we had to run too, so we all said goodbye. Not before Officer Torres added, "Good luck, today, Danny. Tell the truth. Be a hero! Change a life!"

"We really have to go," Ben said, pointing to the bailiff who stood tapping her foot.

"Ready?" Ben asked.

I stood up and looked up at Danny. I let my

tongue droop out.

Danny stretched his hands up to the sky. He breathed in deep.

"One last breath, one last stretch," Danny said.

When the bailiff cleared her throat, I leaned into Danny's legs. My first Life Rule might be to push yourself to do big things, but sometimes we need someone to give us a little push.

Danny took a step forward, and we walked into the courtroom.

CHAPTER 8

The trial went quickly. Not only had Danny seen the guy take the bikes, so had many other people. So, person after person told their stories of how they saw the guy clipping bike locks and dropping them into the back of his shiny red pickup.

When it was Danny's time to testify, I trotted into the "box" with him. Then Judge Mathers reminded people no photos were allowed. We both stretched and sniffed. Then Danny definitely pushed himself by telling what he remembered. Danny answered the questions like a pro. He told the truth. He really was a hero. But the most amazing thing was yet to come.

• • •

Two weeks after the trial, I sat next to Prof. Lester in the professor's lounge.

She had a sandwich that smelled especially nice, so I rested my head on her leg to remind her that I also liked sandwiches. Prof. Lester didn't share even one bite of it.

"This has onion on it, Spooky," she said. "Not good for dogs."

I tried to sneak a bit anyway as she told Reg her big news. Prof. Lester had just learned that the star she discovered, high up in the sky, was officially recognized. Guess what she named it? Spooky! There was going to be a big ceremony with lots of good treats, and I'd get to attend. So, she got a pass on not sharing the sandwich. For now, at least.

Reg's phone vibrated on the table behind me.

He picked it up and clicked.

"Oh, Spooky," he said. "You're gonna want to hear this."

Then he read me the email from Danny.

Dear Spooky,

Mama Caroline is helping me write this letter. She says hi. So does my dad. Thanks again for helping me tell the story and be brave. It's funny because I got nervous about a test last week, and I did your doga pose and sniffed really deep and felt much better.

Here's the other funny thing: Remember how I was so scared to tell the story and so scared of the guy being in court?

Well, I just got a letter from him. He said he was sorry and that he was really thankful that I told my parents about what he was doing. He was really angry at me, he said, all the way up to the trial. But hearing me—this kid, he said—

*tell the truth about what happened changed
something in him. I guess he cried and cried
afterward. He felt so bad. He realized that if I
didn't tell the truth, he would've kept on doing
worse and worse things. He doesn't like being in
jail, but he's glad to be getting some help now.*

*Isn't that weird? I guess Officer Torres was
right. Telling the truth can be scary, but it can
help people. Like you helped Officer Torres and
like you helped me.*

*Gotta run. I've got baseball practice. Can't
wait to see you and meet your pals Sparky,
Penny, Robot, Noodle, and King Tut at the
Helper Hounds picnic next week!*

Love,

Danny

"You did good, Spooky!" Prof. Lester said.
"We're all proud of you."

"Me too," Reg said as he reached over to

scratch my head.

Then he looked at the clock. "Ack, running late again. We gotta go get your gear on."

I would've rather stayed and begged for an onion-less bite of sandwich or maybe a baby carrot, but duty called. So, I stretched and sniffed and off we went.

Spooky's
Life Rules

#1: Push Yourself. Life gets hard. It's easy to give up. Sometimes we just need a tiny, little nudge and doors open or situations change. Don't be afraid to try.

#2: Stretch Yourself. One, stretching is relaxing. But two, stretching literally stretches our muscles. How are you going to reach those muffins on the kitchen counter if you don't stretch a bit? It's the same for anything else in life. Something may seem too high up or too far away for you, but a good stretch will get you there.

#3: Stop to Sniff the Air. Breathing in and out does a few things: it gives us the oxygen we need, it slows our heartbeats, and it helps us relax. This is all super good for our health! Plus, the world is full of interesting, mysterious smells, so our curiosity stirs up as our worries go down.

#4: Share Your Chill. When you feel good or happy or relaxed, share that spirit with others by offering a smile or licking the bacon grease off their sleeves!

Officer Torres'
Life Rules

Change Someone's Life – and let your life be changed. There are lots of ways we can change someone's life for the better: We can tell the truth, we can be kind, we can be forgiving, and we can be helpful to someone. These are all good things! But we should also allow other people to change our lives for the better. Sometimes this means admitting we're wrong or saying we're sorry. It's hard, but it makes for the best life!

FUN FACTS

About American Staffordshire terriers

In this story, Spooky is mistaken for a pit bull. Many people think that Staffordshire Terriers and pit bulls are the same. But that is not true at all!

American Staffordshire terriers have been around for a long time. They became an official breed when registered with the American Kennel Club in 1936. This dog was created by mixing a few different breeds. The most important were the bulldog, the fox terrier, and the much larger mastiff. Over time, and with lots of breeding, these dogs combined to create the Staffordshire terrier, which is often called by its nickname, the "Staffie."

In the past, Staffordshire terriers were used in cruel sports like dog fighting and bear baiting. Yes, these dogs were actually made to attack and fight bears and sometimes bulls! Because of this background, many people think Staffies are aggressive and dangerous. But that could not be further from the truth.

In fact, just like Spooky in the story, most Staffies are affectionate and sweet. They are also very strong. With an average height of 18 inches and a weight between 50 and 80 pounds, these dogs are pure muscle. Because they are strong and smart, in the past, these dogs were trained to help hunters, and also to work on farms, and as guard dogs.

Here's a fun fact: These dogs have a British cousin! In England the breed is also called Staffordshire terrier. These dogs are smaller than their American cousins, but were also used as fighting dogs and working dogs in the past.

Today, a Staffie's best job is as a family pet. These smart, sweet, loyal dogs make great companions and protectors. Some are also trained to work as therapy dogs, just like Spooky. American Staffordshire terriers can truly be a boy's or girl's best friend.

HELPER HOUNDS

If you loved reading about Spooky, you should discover the other five Helper Hounds!

Check with your favorite bookstore or library

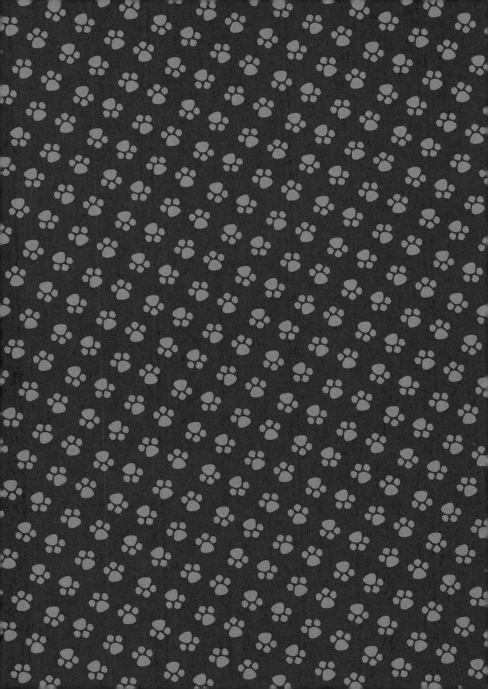